Dirty Bertie

KISS!

D0368236

For the lovely Lauren Ace ~ D R

For Ted – may you always have a BFF ~ A M

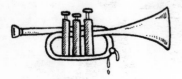

STRIPES PUBLISHING
An imprint of Magi Publications
1 The Coda Centre, 189 Munster Road,
London SW6 6AW

A paperback original
First published in Great Britain in 2011

Characters created by David Roberts
Text copyright © Alan MacDonald, 2011
Illustrations copyright © David Roberts, 2011

ISBN: 978-1-84715-156-8

Printed and bound in the UK.

10 9 8 7 6 5 4 3 2

Dirty Bertie

KISS!

DAVID ROBERTS WRITTEN BY ALAN MACDONALD

Collect all the Dirty Bertie books!

Contents

KISS!

CHAPTER 1

It was morning break. Bertie reached
into his pocket for his secret weapon:
a slimy slug. Unlike most people, Bertie
liked slugs. He liked their sluggy colour
and the cold, slippery feel of them.
He looked around the playground.
Who would be his first victim? Royston
Rich? Royston was always bragging that

nothing scared him. Or Know-All Nick? Bertie would enjoy putting a slug down his neck. But Nick would only tell tales to Miss Boot. He had a better idea – what about Angela Nicely? Angela lived next door to Bertie and she'd been in love with him for ever. She was always telling people that he was her boyfriend. Well, he'd soon put a stop to that. Wait till Angela saw the fat, slimy slug he'd got for her. How she'd scream and beg for mercy!

♥   ♥   ♥

Angela was sitting on a bench, playing a game with her friends, Laura and Maisie.

"Your go, Laura," said Maisie. "Truth, Dare, Kiss or Promise?"

"Truth," said Laura.

Dirty Bertie

"Is it true … I'm your Best Friend Forever?" said Maisie.

Laura thought hard. "No," she said. "Angela is."

Maisie sulked.

"My go, my go!" sang Angela, excitedly.

"Okay," said Laura. "Truth, Dare, Kiss or Promise?"

Angela smiled. "KISS!" she said.

"ANGELA!" squealed Laura and Maisie. "You'll have to kiss a boy!"

"I don't care!" declared Angela.

"All right, but you've got to kiss whoever we say," said Maisie.

"That's the rules," agreed Laura. "Or else you're out of the game."

Maisie looked around the playground for a likely victim. It had to be someone disgusting – some grubby, bogey-nosed boy.

"OH, ANG-ELA!" yelled Bertie, holding up the slug. "Look what I've got!"

Maisie grinned. "HIM!" she said, pointing.

"Yes, Bertie, kiss Bertie!" cried Laura.

Bertie turned pale. His mouth fell open. "W-what?"

"ANGELA WANTS TO KISS YOU!" chanted the girls.

Dirty Bertie

"No she doesn't!" gasped Bertie.

"Yes I do!" beamed Angela, jumping to her feet. "I've got to. It's the rules!"

Bertie turned pink. He backed away. What rules? Had they all gone mad?

"Keep back!" he cried. "I've got a slug!"

"I don't care!" said Angela, coming closer.

"A big wet, slimy slug," said Bertie, holding it out. "I'll put it in your hair!"

But Angela just kept coming. "I'm going to kiss you!" she sang.

"No!" gasped Bertie.

"Yes I am!"

"Go on, Angela!" urged Laura.

"Keep back!" yelled Bertie, desperately.
"Don't come near me!"

Angela took no notice. She puckered
her lips and leaned in closer.

"ARGHHHHHHH!" yelled Bertie.
He dropped the slug and ran for it.

CHAPTER 2

Darren and Eugene were sitting on the wall at the far end of the playground.

"Quick!" panted Bertie, tearing round the corner. "Help me hide!"

"What's going on?" asked Darren.

"She's after me!"

"Who? Miss Boot?"

"No! Angela!"

Dirty Bertie

They both stared at him. "Angela?" said Eugene. "Angela in Class 1?"

"You don't understand," said Bertie. "She wants to…" He could hardly bring himself to say it. "She wants to *kiss* me!"

"KISS YOU!" howled Darren and Eugene.

"Shh! Don't tell everyone!" groaned Bertie.

"But *kiss* you! Ha ha! Hee hee!" chortled his friends, helpless with laughter.

Dirty Bertie

"It's not funny!" groaned Bertie. "She won't leave me alone! Don't let her find me!"

"You better hide then," grinned Darren. "Here she comes."

Bertie dived behind a tub of flowers. A moment later, Angela and her friends came running up.

"Have you seen Bertie?" asked Angela, breathlessly.

Darren looked at Eugene. "Let me think ... have we seen Bertie?"

Eugene frowned. "I don't think so."

"Why do you want him?" asked Darren.

Angela beamed. "I'm going to kiss him!"

"It's the rules!" Laura explained. "She has to, don't you, Angela?"

Angela nodded. She didn't mind kissing Bertie. After all, he was her boyfriend.

"Oh, *you're* Angela," said Darren.
"Bertie's always talking about you, isn't
he, Eugene?"

"Er ... yeah," said Eugene. "He loves
you."

"He wants to marry you!" said Darren.

Angela stared. "Really? He said that?"

"Millions of times," said Darren. "But
you know what he'd like best?"

Angela shook her head.

"A big fat kiss!" said Darren.

Angela clapped her hands. "I'm going to!" she said. "I'm going to kiss him as soon as I find him! Come on!"

She ran off, with her two friends chasing behind.

"Ha ha! Hee hee!" hooted Darren and Eugene, holding their sides.

Bertie crept out from his hiding place. "What did you tell her that for? Now she thinks I like her!"

"No," grinned Darren. "She thinks you LOVE her."

"And you want to marry her!" said Eugene.

Bertie held his head. "Stop saying that! I DON'T!"

"Yes, you *do*! Bertie loves Angela!

Dirty Bertie

Bertie loves Angela!" chanted Darren and Eugene.

"SHUT UP!" yelled Bertie. What if people heard? This was growing worse by the minute.

"Look! There he is!" cried a shrill voice. "BERTIE!"

Bertie turned. *Help!* Angela had spotted him. *RUN!*

♥   ♥   ♥

Bertie screeched round a corner and ducked into the boys' toilets. He darted into one of the cubicles, locking the door behind him. *Phew! Made it!* Angela and her friends had chased him all over the playground – but they couldn't follow him in here. He slumped against the wall, his heart beating fast.

Dirty Bertie

This is a nightmare, he thought. *What if she catches me?* Angela was only small, but she was extremely determined. Imagine it – Bertie, the Terror of Class 3, kissed by a girl. YUCK! It was too horrible for words. He'd never be able to show his face again.

CREAK!

The door of the boys' toilets opened. Bertie froze in terror. Surely it couldn't be Angela?

Footsteps crossed the floor.

CLUMP! CLUMP! CLUMP!

They stopped right outside his door. Bertie held his breath.

RATTLE! RATTLE!

Someone tried the door handle.
Bertie shrank back against the wall.

"BERTIE!" boomed a voice. "I KNOW
YOU'RE IN THERE!"

Bertie sagged with relief. Even facing
the wrath of Miss Boot was better than
being kissed by Angela!

"Just going to the toilet, Miss!" he called.

"Well, get a move on. The bell went
five minutes ago!"

CHAPTER 3

Back in class, Bertie tried to stay calm.
Angela couldn't get him here. He was
safe until lunchtime, and by then she
might have forgotten the whole thing.
He leaned over and tried to sneak a
look at Eugene's answer sheet.

"BERTIE!"

He looked up. Miss Boot was

Dirty Bertie

beckoning him forward.

"Uh oh, trouble," murmured Darren.

Bertie trailed out to the front. What had he done this time? Miss Boot pointed to a pile of books on her desk.

"Take these to Miss Darling," she said.

Bertie brightened up – anything was better than maths. But wait a minute, didn't Miss Darling teach Class 1? That was Angela's class!

"Can't someone else go?" he begged. "I've got a bad leg."

"You were fine just now," snapped Miss Boot.

"But Miss…"

"No arguments, Bertie. And make sure you come straight back."

Huh! He certainly wouldn't be hanging around – not if Angela was nearby.

Dirty Bertie

♥ ♥ ♥

Five minutes later he knocked on the door of Class 1.

"Come in!" called Miss Darling.

Bertie tottered in, trying not to drop the books.

"Miss Boot said to bring you these."

"Thank you, Bertie." Miss Darling smiled. "Put them in the storeroom, can you?"

But Bertie wasn't listening. Someone at the back of the class was waving to him. Angela Nicely. Bertie felt hot. He thought he might pass out.

"Are you all right?" asked Miss Darling. "The books, Bertie. Put them away."

"Oh yes, right." Bertie hurried over to the storeroom. Inside he flicked on the light. Rows of shelves were stacked with hundreds of books.

CLICK!

He spun round. Someone had come in, and shut the door. *Help!* Angela and her friends. Bertie backed towards the shelves. He was trapped!

"Hello, Bertie!" smiled Angela.

"Keep back!" warned Bertie.

"It's your girlfriend," said Maisie. "She just wants one little kiss."

"BLECH!" said Bertie.

"You love her," said Laura. "You want to marry her!"

"I'd rather marry a slug!" replied Bertie.

Dirty Bertie

Dirty Bertie

Angela kept coming – insults had no effect.

"Stay back or I'll … I'll burp!" threatened Bertie.

"I don't care!" said Angela. "I'm going to kiss you!"

Bertie looked around for some kind of weapon. There was nothing but books. He jumped on to a chair. Angela grabbed him round the legs. She pulled. Bertie wobbled. The chair tipped and he lost his balance.

"ARGHHHH!"

THUD! BANG! THUMP!

Bertie sprawled on the floor under a pile of books. The storeroom door flew open and Miss Darling appeared.

"What's going on in here?" she cried, glaring at the three girls.

"Angela, I'm surprised at you! Are you
meant to be in here?"

Angela hung her head. "No, Miss."

"Then get back to your work. And
Bertie, clear up this mess and return to
your class."

"Yes, Miss. Thank you, Miss," said Bertie,
gratefully. He picked himself up. It had
been a close call, but he had survived.

CHAPTER 4

Bertie checked the clock. It had been a long day. Every time he turned a corner, Angela seemed to be lying in wait. At lunch-break he'd avoided her by staying close to Miss Boot. But now it was almost home time. Angela and her friends would be waiting for him outside. His only chance was to make a quick getaway.

Dirty Bertie

DRRINGGG!

The bell went. Bertie shot out of his place. He streaked for the door like a greyhound.

"BERTIE!" barked Miss Boot. "WHERE DO YOU THINK YOU'RE GOING?"

"Home, Miss."

"Did I say you could go?"

"No, but—"

"Then sit down and wait till you're told."

Darren and Eugene grinned as Bertie drooped back to his seat. Miss Boot droned on about homework. By the time she finished it was too late. Through the window, Bertie could see Angela and her pals guarding the gates.

He slunk into the cloakroom and hid behind the coat racks.

"What are you doing?" asked Eugene.

"Hiding. From Angela!" hissed Bertie.

"Your girlfriend?" said Darren.

"It's not funny!" grumbled Bertie. "You should help me, instead of making stupid jokes."

"I'd like to," said Darren, "but I've got to get back. Mum's getting me new trainers. Tell you what, I'll come round later to check you made it home alive," he said.

Eugene hung back. "Are you coming, Bertie?"

"I can't," said Bertie. "She'll see me!"

"Not if you sneak past her," said Eugene. "You could wear a disguise."

A *disguise*, thought Bertie – it wasn't

such a bad idea. But what? He looked around. Someone had left a coat hanging on one of the pegs. He tried it on. He was only going to borrow it … after all, this was an emergency.

♥   ♥   ♥

Five minutes later, Eugene and Bertie crossed the playground. Bertie's face was hidden by a bright pink anorak. He felt ridiculous.

"This had better work," he whispered.

"It will, trust me," said Eugene. "Just don't say a word."

They reached the gates. Angela and her pals blocked their path.

"Have you seen Bertie?" asked Angela.

"Er, no," said Eugene. "He must've gone home."

Dirty Bertie

Angela shook her head. "He hasn't come out yet. We've been watching." She stared at the girl in the pink anorak. "Have *you* seen him?"

Bertie shook his head, keeping it lowered.

"She's a bit shy," explained Eugene.

"What's her name?"

"Er … Tina," said Eugene.

Dirty Bertie

"I'm Angela," said Angela. "When Bertie comes out I'm going to kiss him."

"No chance," muttered Bertie.

"Pardon?"

"She said, 'Oh pants, we'd better go!'" replied Eugene. "Come on, Tina!"

Angela watched them hurry past. She noticed Tina was wearing muddy trainers – just like Bertie's. Come to think of it, she walked like Bertie too. Angela ran after her and pulled down her hood.

"BERTIE!" she squawked.

"Quick!" yelled Bertie. "RUN!"

Dirty Bertie

♥   ♥   ♥

Back home, Bertie leaned against the
front door, panting for breath. Angela
would have caught him this time, if he
hadn't been too fast for her. He thumped
upstairs and threw himself on his bed. No
way was any girl going to kiss him. They'd
have to catch him first, and he was way
too clever. Bertie smiled to himself as he
reached for his secret stash of biscuits.

He was munching the last one when
the doorbell rang.

"Bertie, it's for you!" yelled his sister,
Suzy. "It's one of your friends!"

"Send them up," shouted Bertie. It was
probably Darren come to make fun of
him. Ha! Wait till he told him about his
brilliant escape.

Dirty Bertie

The door opened. Bertie looked up.

"Hello, Bertie!" beamed Angela. "All on your own?"

HAMSTER!

CHAPTER 1

Bertie yawned and glanced at the clock. Ten minutes to go. Tomorrow was the start of the half-term holidays.

Over by the window Snuffles, the class hamster, dozed in his cage. Snuffles was a legend. Miss Boot said he was six years old, which for a hamster was like a hundred or something. If he lived much

longer he'd probably make it into the
Guinness World Records. It was just a pity
he slept so much of the time. Bertie
reckoned it was because he was bored.
Anyone would be bored having to listen
to Miss Boot every day. If Snuffles was
Bertie's pet he would have taught him
tricks – rolling over, standing on his head,
maybe even tightrope walking.

Dirty Bertie

Bertie sighed. It was pointless even thinking about it – Miss Boot would never trust him with Snuffles. Over the holidays the class took it in turns to look after the hamster, but Miss Boot only chose "sensible" children. She had pinned a list of names on the wall. Eugene was on the list, so was Donna and Know-All Nick. Bertie wasn't. It wasn't fair. Why did he never get picked for anything?

DRRINGGG!

The bell rang for home time. Everyone cheered and packed away their books.

"Wait!" boomed Miss Boot. "Who is taking Snuffles home for the holidays?"

Donna raised her hand. "It's Eugene's turn, Miss."

"Ah, yes," said Miss Boot. "Wait behind please, Eugene."

The class piled out of the door. Bertie waited with Eugene while Miss Boot collected together Snuffles' things.

"Don't forget to clean out his cage and give him food and water every day," said Miss Boot.

"Yes… Oh no!" Eugene gasped.

"What's the matter?" asked Miss Boot.

"I just remembered – we're away this week visiting my gran."

Miss Boot rolled her eyes. "Isn't anyone staying at home?"

Eugene shook his head.

"Really! Why didn't you say so before?" asked Miss Boot.

"I forgot," said Eugene.

"Well, who's going to look after Snuffles? We can't leave him here – and everyone's gone home."

Dirty Bertie

"I haven't!" said Bertie, eagerly.

Miss Boot glared. "*You?*"

"Yes, I could look after him."

"But you haven't asked your parents," said Miss Boot. "What if they say no?"

"They won't," Bertie replied. "My mum loves pets!"

This wasn't strictly true, but Bertie wasn't going to let a little thing like that get in the way. This might be his only chance to look after Snuffles.

"Please!" he begged.

Miss Boot groaned. Why Bertie, of all people?

"Very well," she said. "But I am trusting you, Bertie. I've had Snuffles a long time and if anything happened to him I'd be very upset. *Very* upset."

"I'll guard him with my life, Miss," promised Bertie.

"Mind you do," said Miss Boot.

Bertie hurried out, before his teacher changed her mind. At last! Snuffles was his – for a whole week!

Dirty Bertie

CHAPTER 2

CREAK, CREAK, CREAK!

Bertie crept up the stairs, carrying the hamster cage. Now that he'd got Snuffles home, he was beginning to worry. What if Miss Boot was right? What if his mum said no?

"Bertie?" called Mum. "Is that you?"

Uh oh. Bertie turned round, hiding the

cage behind his back. Mum was at the bottom of the stairs.

"What are you doing?" she demanded.

"Nothing. Just going to my room."

Mum narrowed her eyes. "What's that you've got?"

"Where?"

"Behind your back. I'm not blind, Bertie."

"Just … school stuff."

"Show me," said Mum.

Bertie swallowed hard. There was no escape. He brought out the cage and removed the jumper covering it.

Mum groaned. "Bertie! Is that a HAMSTER?"

"No!" said Bertie. "Well, only a little one."

"Where on earth did you get it?"

"From school," Bertie replied. "I was

specially chosen to look after him."

Mum folded her arms. "I told you no more pets," she said. "Whiffer's quite enough trouble."

"But a hamster's different," argued Bertie. "He won't be any trouble."

"No, because we're not keeping him," said Mum.

"Please! It's only for a week."

"No! He'll have to go back."

Dirty Bertie

"He can't! School's closed. If I don't keep him, he's got nowhere to go."

Snuffles gazed up at them with large, sad eyes.

Mum sighed heavily. "All right! But just for a week!"

"Yesssssss!" cried Bertie.

"But he stays in your bedroom," said Mum. "And it's your job to look after him."

"I will!" promised Bertie.

"And don't let him out of his cage."

Bertie gaped. "He'll have to come out sometimes. He needs exercise!"

"We've got a dog!" said Mum. "What happens if Whiffer gets hold of him? I'm not phoning Miss Boot to say her hamster's been eaten!"

Bertie sighed. "Okay, I'll be careful."

He carried the cage up to his room, shutting the door on Whiffer, who was eager to see what was inside.

He'd keep Snuffles in his cage ... at least most of the time. He would only let him out for something important – like learning tricks for instance.

CHAPTER 3

Bertie was eager to get started, but he soon found out that hamsters weren't as much fun as he'd expected.

He began by drawing up a list of tricks to work on. Next he made an obstacle course out of toilet roll tubes and biscuit tins. But Snuffles slept all day and showed no interest. Bertie tried to tempt him out with bits of carrot.

Next day he tried to train Snuffles to balance on top of a ball. Snuffles fell off.

Suzy said he was wasting his time. "Hamsters are nocturnal," she said, "they only come out at night."

Bertie soon discovered this for himself. Snuffles kept him awake every night running round in his wheel. On top of that, Bertie had to keep his door closed, because Whiffer was always whining and trying to get in. By Sunday evening, he was exhausted. Hamsters were so much work!

"Have you cleaned out Snuffles' cage today?" asked Mum, over supper.

"Yes!" groaned Bertie.

"Well, it's dirty again! He does his business in there!"

"EWW! GROSS!" cried Suzy, pulling a face.

"It's only poo," said Bertie. "You can see them in the cage, they're like tiny black sausages…"

"MUM, tell him!" cried Suzy, putting down her fork.

Mum rolled her eyes. "Bertie, please! We're trying to eat!"

"I was only saying," grumbled Bertie.

"Well, never mind the details," said Dad. "Just clean out his cage."

"Can't I do it in the morning?"

"No," said Mum, firmly. "I want that cage spotless tonight."

After supper, Bertie stomped upstairs. *It's not fair,* he thought. *People have to clean up their own poo, so why can't hamsters?* He opened the cage door. Snuffles was awake. He darted around, getting in the way. Bertie took him out and carried him over to his beanbag.

Dirty Bertie

Snuffles crawled around, glad to be free at last.

"You stay there," Bertie told him. "This won't take long."

Ten minutes later, the cage was done. Bertie turned round to get Snuffles.

Yikes! Where did he go?

Bertie grabbed the beanbag but there were no hamsters underneath. He looked around, starting to panic. *Keep calm*, he thought. *He can't have gone far.* He looked under the bed. Nothing. Nothing behind the curtains or the bookcase, either. Bertie turned round.

ARGHHHHH! The bedroom door was open! Snuffles could have wandered out. He could be anywhere!

"Bertie!" called Mum. "Have you finished doing that cage?"

"Um … almost!" Bertie shouted.

Dirty Bertie

"Well, as soon as you have, can you bring me your dirty washing?"

"Okay!" Bertie slumped on to his beanbag. What on earth was he going to do? Mum would go bananas if she found out. He wouldn't tell her – not yet. He just needed time to find Snuffles and get him back in his cage. A search party – that was it. He hurried to the phone.

Soon after, Darren arrived. The two of them searched the house from top to bottom. But there was no sign of Snuffles. Not even a tiny trail of hamster poo.

"Boy, you are in big trouble!" said Darren, as they went out into the garden. "Miss Boot will go up the wall. She'll murder you!"

Darren's right, thought Bertie. Miss Boot

was fonder of Snuffles than she was of most of her class. Bertie had heard her talking to him in a soppy, baby voice.

"He must be somewhere. Keep looking!" he said.

"And what about us?" Darren went on. "He was our hamster too. I'm going to miss him!"

"Then help me find him!" said Bertie.

Whiffer was dozing under the garden bench. He yawned contentedly.

"Darren," said Bertie. "You don't think…?"

Darren looked at Whiffer. "Naaa! Don't be stupid! He wouldn't!"

"No," agreed Bertie. All the same, Whiffer would chase anything – squirrels especially. And to a dog, a fluffy hamster looked much like a squirrel. What if

Dirty Bertie

Whiffer had chased Snuffles? What if he had caught him and… Bertie couldn't bear to think about it. Everyone at school would blame him!

"What are we going to do?" he moaned.

Darren shrugged. "Don't ask me! You're the one who lost him!"

"But what if we can't find him?"

"You'll just have to face Miss Boot.
Or else buy another one."

Another hamster! thought Bertie. *That's
not such a bad idea.* He could look in
the pet shop for one like Snuffles. There
was just one problem.

"I don't have any money," he said.

They were silent for a while, lost in
thought. Suddenly Bertie leaped to his
feet.

"We could make one!" he cried.

"What?"

"A hamster –
out of fur 'n' stuff.
You know, like a
teddy bear."

Darren snorted.

"Miss Boot won't fall for that. It'll just sit
there like a blob."

"That won't matter!" said Bertie. "We'll just say he's asleep. Snuffles is always asleep!"

Darren considered it. "But what about him eating?"

"*We'll* feed him," said Bertie. "The two of us. We'll just pretend and stuff the food in our pockets."

"It'll never work," said Darren. "Miss Boot will find out."

"Not if we're careful. Anyway, it's only till I can save up for a new one."

Darren still looked doubtful. It sounded potty to him. Trying to pass off some stuffed bit of fur as Snuffles? But Bertie was convinced it would work – and besides, they didn't have a better idea.

CHAPTER 4

Monday morning arrived – the first day back at school. Class 3 trooped into their room under the stern eye of Miss Boot. Bertie tried to sneak past, carrying Snuffles' cage.

"BERTIE!" barked Miss Boot.

Uh oh. Bertie stopped in his tracks.

"I'll just, er, put Snuffles back," he said.

"Come here!" said Miss Boot. "I want to check that he's all right."

Bertie plodded over miserably.

"I hope you looked after him properly," said Miss Boot. "Did you feed him every day, and clean out his cage?"

"Yes, yes," said Bertie. "Can I put him back now?"

"Wait," said Miss Boot. "I haven't seen him yet."

Bertie's heart sank. This was just what he'd been dreading. The class crowded round, eager to get a glimpse of their favourite hamster. Bertie set down the cage.

"Where is he?" asked Miss Boot.

"There," said Bertie. "He's asleep."

All Miss Boot could see was a furry lump, hidden under piles of straw.

"He looks fatter," she frowned.

"No, I don't think so," said Bertie.

"What have you been feeding him?"

"Just the usual hamster stuff."

Miss Boot prodded the furry lump with her finger. "He's not moving!" she squawked.

Bertie gulped. He got ready to run.

Miss Boot gave Snuffles another prod. He slumped on his side.

"Ohhh!" The children gasped.

Miss Boot reached into the cage and brought Snuffles out. She stared at the rolled-up sock covered in sticky fur. It had a lopsided smile and two goggly eyes.

"BERTIE!" thundered Miss Boot. "WHAT DO YOU CALL THIS?"

Bertie turned very pale. "Crumbs," he said. "I've been looking for that sock."

WHAM!

The front door slammed shut. Bertie drooped into the kitchen and threw his bag on the floor. Mum was sorting through a pile of wet washing.

"Good day at school?" she asked.

"Terrible," groaned Bertie, flopping into a chair.

"Did you take Snuffles back?" asked Mum.

"Oh, um, yeah, of course."

"Really? I expect Miss Boot was pleased to see him?"

"Yes, very pleased," said Bertie.

"That's funny," said Mum. "Because when I checked through your dirty washing basket I found something."

64

Dirty Bertie

She pointed to a cardboard box on the worktop.

Bertie went over. He looked inside.

"SNUFFLES!" he cried. "YOU'RE ALIVE!"

"No thanks to you," said Mum.
"He could have ended up in the washing machine. Why didn't you tell me he'd got out?"

"I thought you might be cross," said Bertie.

He scooped up Snuffles and cuddled him. He never thought he'd be so pleased to see him.

"Clever boy," he grinned. "Wait till I tell Miss Boot."

Mum smiled. "Well, he certainly seems pleased to see you."

"How can you tell?" asked Bertie.

"Because he's just pooed on your jumper."

CHAPTER 1

It was Saturday morning. Mum was tidying the kitchen. Bertie was still in his dressing gown, eating breakfast. "Listen," he said. "I can burp my name…"

He took a deep breath.

"*BURPIE!*"

Mum groaned. "Bertie! Please!"

"What? I bet you can't do it."

Dirty Bertie

"I don't want to," said Mum. "It's disgusting!"

Bertie didn't see why. At school he was the champion burper of his class. He'd been practising for weeks. His longest burp was a record-breaking six seconds.

"Get dressed," said Mum. "Mrs Smugly's coming and she's bringing Flora."

Bertie groaned. "FLORA? What for?"

"Because I invited her mum for coffee."

"You don't even like her!" grumbled Bertie.

"Of course I do!"

"You don't!" said Bertie. "You told Dad she's stuck up and she never stops boasting about Flora."

Mum wiped the table. "Well, Flora is very talented. You should try to be more like her."

Dirty Bertie

"Huh! No thanks!" said Bertie, scornfully. Who wanted to be like goody-goody Flora? Last time she came he'd had to sit through hours of her playing the clarinet. The way her mum went on, you'd think she was some kind of genius. *Anyway*, thought Bertie, *I bet Flora can't burp for six seconds.*

DING DONG!

"They're here," groaned Mum. "For heaven's sake, Bertie, get dressed."

Bertie stomped up to his room. He got changed as slowly as he could. But then he remembered the chocolate biscuits that Mum always kept for visitors. He hurried downstairs.

Dirty Bertie

There were only three biscuits left on the plate. Bertie helped himself as he sat down.

"And how is Flora doing at school?" asked Mum.

"Oh, wonderfully!" said Mrs Smugly. "She came top in maths again, didn't you darling?"

Flora nodded. She eyed Bertie and took a biscuit, leaving only one.

"As for ballet, Miss Leotard says she's quite outstanding," said Mrs Smugly. "Does Bertie go to ballet?"

"Er, no, not really," said Mum.

Bertie scowled. Did he look like he went to ballet?

Mrs Smugly chattered on. "Of course, it's hard to fit it all in. Ballet on Saturdays, clarinet Mondays, French classes Tuesday. Does Bertie speak French?"

"Not yet," said Mum. "I'm sure he will."

"Perhaps when he's older," said Mrs Smugly. "Flora's lucky – she's just so gifted. What a pity we didn't bring her clarinet."

"Mmm. What a pity," yawned Mum.

Bertie reached for the last chocolate biscuit. It was gone! Who had swiped it? Flora smiled sweetly and stuck out a sticky tongue at him.

"And what about you, Bertie?" asked Mrs Smugly.

"Mmm?" said Bertie.

"How's the trumpet?"

Bertie looked blank. *Trumpet? What trumpet?*

"You know, Bertie," said Mum, nodding at him. "Actually he's doing very well. He's taking Grade 5, aren't you, Bertie?"

Bertie stared. *Grade 5? Taking it where?*

Mrs Smugly raised her eyebrows. "Grade 5? That is impressive. I'd love to hear you play sometime, Bertie."

So would I, thought Bertie. His mum was avoiding his eye. There was definitely something funny going on.

Frrrp
Prrrp
PLLLth

CHAPTER 2

That evening over supper Bertie
mentioned what had happened.

"She told them WHAT?" said Dad.

"That I play the trumpet," repeated
Bertie. "It turns out I'm really good."

"YOU? Play the trumpet?" hooted Suzy.

Mum had gone rather red. "Um,
anyone for more potato?" she asked.

Dirty Bertie

"But you don't even play an instrument!" said Dad.

"I do! I play the recorder!"

"Once," said Dad. "Until you broke it." He looked at Mum. "But what on earth made you say he plays the trumpet?"

Mum turned redder still. She wished Bertie had kept quiet.

"I had to say something," she sighed. "I was sick of hearing about fabulous Flora. I just mentioned that Bertie likes music."

"LIKES MUSIC?" cried Bertie. "You told them I play the *trumpet*!"

"Well, you might. You must be good at something."

"I am!" said Bertie. "I can burp for six whole seconds!"

"In any case," said Dad, ignoring him.
"You'll have to explain it's not true."

"I can't do that now," said Mum. "It will
look as if I told a lie."

"You did!" laughed Suzy.

"Well yes, but only to Mrs Smugly, and
she'll never find out."

BRINGG! BRINGG!

The phone rang. Mum hurried to
answer it, glad to escape. But when she
returned she looked rather pale.

"That was Barbara Smugly," she said.
"She asked if Bertie could play in a
concert, with the Pudsley Junior
Orchestra."

"HA HA!" howled Suzy. "Imagine that!"

"I hope you said 'no'?" said Dad.

Mum bit her lip. "Not exactly. I sort
of agreed."

Dirty Bertie

PLUUUUUUGHHHHH!
A lump of mash flew
from Bertie's mouth.

"WHAT?" he gasped.

"I'm sorry," said Mum.
"I couldn't get out of it! She'd
already put your name down."

"A concert?" cried Bertie. "But I don't
play the trumpet! I haven't even got one!"

"We'll hire one from a shop," said
Mum, desperately. "It won't be so bad.
Just a few rehearsals."

Rehearsals! This was getting worse and
worse! Well, he wouldn't do it. After all,
none of this was his fault.

"You can't be serious," said Dad.
"They'll find out he can't play."

"They won't," said Mum. "It's an
orchestra. There'll be dozens of children.

Who's going to notice if Bertie isn't playing?"

"No one," answered Bertie. "Cos I'm not doing it."

"You have to!" pleaded Mum. "I've promised."

"No way!" said Bertie.

Mum sighed. She'd dug herself into a deep hole. If Bertie backed out now, Mrs Smugly would want to know why. And what if she found out the truth? No, Bertie would just have to go through with it, and there was one way to persuade him.

"Bertie, you know that restaurant you like?" said Mum.

Bertie gasped. "Pizza Pronto?" Pizza Pronto served the biggest, yummiest pizzas in the world.

Dirty Bertie

"Yes. There's one opposite the concert hall."

"Can we go? Please!" begged Bertie.

"Okay," said Mum. "As long as you play in the concert."

Bertie hesitated. This was bribery. On the other hand it was the best pizza in the world.

"It's a deal," he said.

Dad groaned. Bertie playing the trumpet – in a concert? This could only end in disaster.

CHAPTER 3

Rehearsals took place every Tuesday at
Pudsley Hall. When Bertie arrived for his
first practice the other children were
seated on the stage. They clutched violins,
flutes, trombones and tubas. A girl
struggled with a cello twice her size.
Bertie looked round for somewhere to sit.
He spotted Flora practising her clarinet.

Dirty Bertie

"Hello," he said, sitting down.

"You can't sit there," said Flora, rudely.

"Why not?"

"*Duh!* You're with the trumpets. Over there with Nigel."

Bertie clambered over chairs and music stands to reach his place. There were two boys, both holding shiny trumpets. The one called Nigel wore a velvet bow tie.

"Hello, I'm Bertie," said Bertie, sitting down.

"You can't sit there," snapped Nigel.

"Why not?"

Dirty Bertie

"That's for first trumpets. Second trumpets sit behind."

Bertie sighed wearily. "Does it matter?"

"Of course it matters!" said Nigel. "I'm first trumpet because I'm better than you. Why do you think I'm playing the solo?"

Bertie rolled his eyes.

"Go on then! Move!" ordered Nigel.

Bertie moved to the seat behind.

The conductor, Mr Quaver, arrived. He droned on about the music they were going to play. Bertie yawned. He got his trumpet out. Surely it couldn't be that difficult to play? He took a deep breath.

Pffft! Pfffft!

Not a sound. He tried again, holding down the keys. Nothing.

Dirty Bertie

Then he noticed a small key he hadn't
yet tried. Bertie pressed it. A glob of spit
dripped on the floor.

Wow! thought Bertie. *A dribble key!*

Mr Quaver finished talking and asked
them to open their music. Bertie stared
at the page – it was covered with
squiggly black tadpoles.

Mr Quaver tapped his stand. He raised
his baton and the orchestra began to play.
The violins scraped. The flutes tootled.
The drums boomed. Nigel and the others
raised their trumpets. Bertie copied.

PAA PA-PA PA PAAA!

Pfft! Pfft! went Bertie, not getting a note.

The trumpets rested. The music went
on. Bertie noticed Nigel raise his
trumpet, ready for his solo. Bertie leaned
forward and pressed his dribble key.

Dirty Bertie

Dirty Bertie

"EWWWWWW!" howled Nigel, leaping to his feet.

"What on earth's the matter?" asked the conductor.

"Something dribbled down my neck!" Nigel swung round, glaring at Bertie. Bertie smiled back.

"Nigel!" sighed Mr Quaver. "Can we please get on?"

Bertie sat back in his seat and smiled. Maybe rehearsals wouldn't be so bad after all.

Over the next weeks, Bertie's trumpet practice drove his family mad. At first he couldn't get a note but eventually he got the hang of it. Terrible noises came from his bedroom – parps and poops and

deafening squeaks.
Dad said it
sounded like a
herd of trumping
elephants. Suzy
went about
with her fingers
in her ears. Mum
said she wished
she'd never given Bertie the
trumpet in the first place. One
evening she decided they needed to have
a talk.

"Bertie," she said, "it's nice you want
to practise, but I'm not asking you to
actually play in the concert."

Bertie shrugged. "It's okay. I want to."

"Yes, but it's better if you don't."

"Why?" asked Bertie.

Dirty Bertie

"Because, well … you can't really play the trumpet!"

"I was playing just now!" said Bertie.

"Yes, but a concert is different," said Mum. "There's an audience. If you make that horrible noise people will hear!"

"I want them to hear," said Bertie.

"That's the whole point," said Mum. "They'll realize you can't play."

Bertie frowned. "So what you're saying is, I just have to sit there and pretend?"

"Yes," said Mum. "Pretend but don't play."

"Not even a bit?"

"No," said Mum firmly. "Remember, no playing or no Pizza Pronto."

Bertie sighed. There was no pleasing some people – they just didn't appreciate good music.

CHAPTER 4

The night of the big concert finally
arrived. Bertie fiddled nervously with his
clip-on bow tie. He'd never performed
in a concert before. He would be
playing (or not playing) in front of
hundreds of people, including his whole
family. Still, what could possibly go
wrong? All he had to do was pretend.

Dirty Bertie

It was a small price to pay for a Pizza Pronto Cheese Feast pizza.

His family came with him to the dressing room. Mrs Smugly was there brushing Flora's hair.

"Hello, Bertie," she trilled. "I'm so looking forward to hearing you play!"

"Me too!" grinned Suzy.

Mum nudged her to keep quiet.

Just then, Mr Quaver hurried in, looking flustered. "Disaster!" he cried. "Nigel's got a tummy bug! He can't come, and he's playing the solo!"

Mrs Smugly tutted. "Well, surely someone else can do it? What about Bertie?"

"M-ME?" gasped Bertie.

"Yes, your mum's always saying how talented you are. Here's your big chance!"

Mum gulped. "But surely—"

"Splendid! That's settled, then!" interrupted Mr Quaver.

"I'm sure you'll be marvellous!" said Mrs Smugly, patting Bertie on the head.

Bertie felt sick. This wasn't happening! He'd wanted to play his trumpet, but not by himself. How could he play a solo when he could barely manage two notes?

Dirty Bertie

The audience clapped as the Pudsley Junior Orchestra walked onstage. Bertie could see his family in the front row. Gran waved. Suzy gave him a thumbs up. Next to her, Mrs Smugly clapped madly. Bertie glanced at the exits. Maybe if he made a run for it now he could escape? But Mr Quaver was marching onstage and bowing to the audience. He raised

his baton. The concert began.

The violins swelled. The flutes tootled. The drums boomed. Bertie pretended to join in with the trumpets. He was sweating. He should never have let his mum talk him into this. On and on went the music, rising and falling. Suddenly he noticed it had gone very quiet. Mr Quaver's baton was pointing at him. Yikes! The trumpet solo! This was his big moment.

Dirty Bertie

Bertie stood up and raised his trumpet to his lips. He blew.

Pffft! Pfffttt!

Nothing.

Pffft!

Silence.

He blew with all his might. A single note wailed out like a dying bluebottle.

PAAAARRRRRRRPPPP!

The audience gasped. Bertie's mum went bright red. Mrs Smugly looked as if she was going to pass out. Next to her, Gran and Suzy were shaking with laughter.

Bertie lowered his trumpet, bowed and sat down. All in all he felt it hadn't gone too badly. At least he'd still be going to Pizza Pronto.

Dirty Bertie

After the concert, Bertie's family
collected him from the dressing room.

"Come on," hissed Mum. "Let's get out
of here before anyone sees us!"

But at that moment, the door opened
and in walked Mrs Smugly. She bore
down on them like a battleship.

"Never!" she fumed. "Never in my life
have I heard anything so dreadful! Your
son ruined the whole evening!"

Gran grinned. "I quite enjoyed it."

Mrs Smugly ignored her and rounded
on Bertie. "The truth. Have you taken
any music exams?"

"Well, um … no," admitted Bertie.

"And have you ever in your life had a
trumpet lesson?"

Bertie shook his head.

"Just as I thought," snapped Mrs Smugly, glaring at Mum. "He can't speak French, he doesn't go to ballet and he can't play the trumpet. Tell me, is there anything he *can* do?"

"Actually there is," said Bertie. "Do you want to hear?"

He took a deep breath…